The Sycamore Tree

AND OTHER AFRICAN TALES

Retold by Lee Po

Illustrated by Carole Byard

Doubleday & Company, Inc.   Garden City, New York

Text Copyright © 1974 by Lee Po
Illustrations Copyright © 1974 by Carole Byard
All Rights Reserved
Printed in the United States of America
First Edition

Library of Congress Cataloging in Publication Data

Po, Lee.
  The sycamore tree and other African tales.

  CONTENTS: The cracks in Tortoise's shell. — How
Kim-ana-u-eze married the daughter of Sun and Moon. — The
sycamore tree. — The woman who was made of oil. [etc.]
  1. Tales, African. [1. Folklore — Africa]
I. Byard, Carole M., illus. II. Title.
PZ8.1.L368Sy   398.2'0967
ISBN 0-385-00561-X Trade
0-385-02840-7 Prebound
Library of Congress Catalog Card Number 74-755

Contents

The Cracks in Tortoise's Shell

Tortoise was very sad because he could not visit his friend Vulture. Vulture flew to see him almost every day. But Tortoise was never able to return the visits because he had no wings.

"Wife," Tortoise said, "I have to think of a way to visit Vulture. He is my good friend, and I have never been to his house. He must think I am very rude."

"Why would he think you are rude?" Mrs. Tortoise asked. "He knows you have no wings to fly with."

"Even though I have no wings, it is rude."

"But there is nothing to be done," his wife said.

"You could tie me up in a parcel of tobacco. When Vulture comes, ask if he will take the tobacco and use it to buy grain for us."

Mrs. Tortoise did as he asked and put him in the parcel. When Vulture came he asked where Tortoise was. Mrs. Tortoise said he had gone on a journey. She asked Vulture if he would take the tobacco and buy grain for her.

Vulture agreed and flew away with the parcel in his mouth. When he was nearing home, he heard a voice. "It's your friend Tortoise. I've come to visit your house."

Vulture was so surprised that he opened his mouth and let the parcel fall. Tortoise went crashing to earth. His shell cracked to pieces and he died. So the friendship of Vulture and Tortoise was ended. But to this day you can still see the cracks in a tortoise's shell.

ZAMBIA

How Kim-ana-u-eze Married the Daughter of Sun and Moon

Long ago there was a man named Kim-ana-u-eze who wanted to marry the daughter of Lord Sun and Lady Moon. He would not marry any girl who lived on earth.

He wrote a marriage letter, but he could not find anyone to deliver it. Even Vulture could fly only halfway up to the sky.

Then one day Frog came to Kim-ana-u-eze and offered to deliver the letter for him.

"How can you do it?" asked Kim-ana-u-eze. "Even Vulture, who has wings, cannot fly to the sky kingdom."

"Master, I can do it," Frog said. "Give me the letter and I will show you."

Frog put the letter in his mouth. He went and hid in the well where the water girls of Lord Sun came to get their water.

There Frog waited until the girls climbed down a spider web from the sky kingdom. When they dipped their jug into the water, Frog jumped into it. Thus he was able to travel up to the sky.

He jumped out of the jug and placed the letter on a table where Lord Sun would see it. Then he hid. Lord Sun found the letter and read it. He was very puzzled. He wondered who Kim-ana-u-eze was and how he had managed to get the letter up to the sky.

Lord Sun decided to answer the letter. He said he would consider the marriage, but Kim-ana-u-eze must come in person with a present. Lord Sun put the letter on the table and left the room.

Then Frog took the letter in his mouth. He got back in the jug and waited. When the water girls took the jug to the well, Frog jumped out into the water. He waited for the girls to leave. Then he set out to see Kim-ana-u-eze.

Kim-ana-u-eze was surprised and pleased. He wrote another letter to Lord Sun and Lady Moon. He sent some coins with it as a present and said that he was staying on earth to look for a wooing present. Frog came back the next morning. He took the letter and the money, and he went back to the well to wait for the water girls. Thus Frog was once again able to get up to the sky kingdom.

He put the letter and the money on the table. Lord Sun came and read the letter. He wrote an answer telling Kim-ana-u-eze he was pleased with the first present. He said he would accept a sack of money for the wooing present. Frog took the letter to Kim-ana-u-eze the same way he had before.

Now it was time for Kim-ana-u-eze to choose the wedding day. He said to Frog, "Who will bring the bride to earth? You are able to carry the letters, but you cannot fetch Lord Sun's daughter."

But Frog said, "Master, I can do it."

So Kim-ana-u-eze prepared the sack of money and wrote a letter saying he would soon come for his bride.

This time Frog stayed in the sky kingdom. When everyone had gone to sleep, he went to the room where the daughter of Lord Sun slept. He took out both of her eyes and wrapped them in a handkerchief. Then he went back and hid in the jug.

When morning came and the girl could not see, Lord Sun was frightened. He sent for Ngombo, the medicine man. Ngombo said that the girl's intended husband had cast a spell on her.

"Only when she is brought to her new husband will she see again."

When Lord Sun heard this, he ordered the water carriers to take his daughter down to earth. Frog went down as usual in the water jug.

Frog jumped out of the well and spoke to the girl. He returned her eyes and told her he would take her to her husband.

So the daughter of Lord Sun and Lady Moon followed Frog to the house of Kim-ana-u-eze. When they arrived, Kim-ana-u-eze welcomed his new wife and Frog into his house.

ANGOLA

The Sycamore Tree

There was once a woman who was very sad because she had no husband or children. She was lonely and unhappy so she went to the medicine man for help.

"Do you want a husband or children?" the medicine man asked her.

"Children," she said.

"Take your cooking pots," the medicine man said, "and find a fruit-bearing sycamore tree. Fill the pots with fruit and put them in your hut. Then go out for a walk."

The woman did all these things. She was

gone on her walk for a long time. When she came back she heard the sound of children laughing and playing. Her hut was filled with little children waiting to greet her.

Now she was no longer sad and lonely. She was happy living with her children.

But one day she became angry at the children. In her anger, she scolded them for being the children of a tree. The children left her. They went back to the sycamore tree and became fruit again. The woman wept bitterly. She was sad and lonely again. All her beautiful children were gone.

She went back to the medicine man and asked what she could do. He told her he did not know. She wanted to go to the tree with her cooking pots and collect the fruit again. He said it would do no harm to try, but he did not think the magic would work this time.

But the woman was willing to try anything to get her children and her happiness back. She climbed the tree with her cooking pots. When she reached the fruit, they all put forth eyes and stared at her. This frightened her so that she fainted, and her neighbors had to come and take her down from the tree.

Never again did she go to the tree to look for her children.

KENYA

The Woman Who
Was Made of Oil

There was once a woman who was made of oil. She was fat and very beautiful. Many young men wanted to marry her, but her parents always refused. They knew she would melt if she had to work out in the sun.

But there was one young man who would not be discouraged. He was in love with the woman made of oil, and he begged her parents to let her marry him. He promised he would always keep her in the shade. Finally the woman's parents agreed, and the young man took her home with him.

Now he had another wife at home. This first wife became very jealous of the oil woman because she stayed home in the shade instead of helping with the farm work.

The jealous wife made the oil woman feel guilty for not working. One day when their husband was gone, she nagged and nagged until the oil woman finally agreed to go out and help with the work.

On the way to the farm the oil woman tried to stay in the shade. She was very frightened because all her life her mother had told her she would melt away if she stayed in the sun too long. When they got to the farm, she tried to stay in the shade of a tree. But the jealous wife was determined to make her work in the fields. The fat woman's little sister, who had come with her to her husband's house, begged her not to go into the sun. But the oil woman was so tired of listening to the jealous wife that she went out and began to work.

No sooner had she started to work in the heat than she began to melt. She melted very fast. Soon there was nothing left of her but one big toe, which had been covered by a leaf. The little sister was very sad. She carefully picked up the toe, wrapped it in leaves and placed it in the bottom of her basket. When she got home, she put the toe in a pot filled with water.

When the husband came home that night, he wanted to know where his fat wife was. The little girl showed him the pot where the toe was and told him what had happened.

"In three months my sister will come back to life," she said. "But if you do not get rid of your jealous wife, I will return to my mother's house with the pot, so my sister will be safe."

The husband was very angry over what the jealous wife had done. He returned her at once to her parents and got his dowry back. The wife's parents sold her as a servant.

After three months had passed, the little sister opened the pot. The woman of oil came back to life — just as fat and beautiful as she had been before. The husband was so happy he gave a feast for the whole village.

Since that time it has been the custom for a husband to return an evil wife to her parents, who sell her as a servant and give the dowry back to the man so he can buy another wife.

NIGERIA

The Beautiful Girl
Who Had No Teeth

I am a beautiful girl but I have no teeth," the girl sang as she walked along the road.

"What?" yelled her new husband. "Open your mouth and let me see." When she opened her mouth, he saw only a black ridge where the teeth should have been. "No one told me about this. I'm going to take you back to your father."

Only that morning he had given her father five of his finest cattle to buy this girl for his wife. He had been happy to get such a beautiful wife. Now he was bitterly disappointed to find she had no teeth.

They returned to her father's village. He gave the girl back to her father and demanded his cattle.

When he returned home without the girl, his father asked, "Where is your wife, my son?"

"She had no teeth," replied the son. "How could I bring her home?"

The man had two younger brothers, who were also looking for wives. The second son asked his father if he could go look at the girl for himself.

The father agreed, and the second son set out with the five cattle.

When he arrived at the village, he said to the girl's father, "I have come to ask for your daughter in marriage. I have brought you five fine cattle."

The second son and the girl set out on the journey home. After they had gone a little way she began to sing, "I'm a beauti-ful girl, but I have no teeth."

The young man didn't believe her. He asked her to open her mouth and show him. He saw only a black ridge where the teeth should have been. He at once returned to her father and asked for his cattle back.

When he got home, his father asked, "Where is your wife?"

"It was true. She had no teeth," he replied.

The youngest brother now asked if he could go and see for himself. The father agreed.

But the two older brothers asked, "Do you think we are lying? Do you think we are crazy?"

"No," their younger brother said, "but I would like to see a girl who has no teeth."

He went to the father, presented the cattle and asked for the girl.

The old man said, "You are very young

to take a wife. Besides, your brothers already took my daughter and returned her. But you can try if you wish."

The young man set out with his new wife. On the way she began to sing, "I'm a beautiful girl, but I have no teeth."

"Open your mouth," he said. He saw the black ridge. "Well, never mind. Let's be on our way."

Later they stopped at a river to bathe. She began to sing the same song.

While they were bathing, he grabbed her around the neck and told her to open her mouth. Then he began scrubbing her mouth with sand. Soon he found a set of beautiful teeth beneath the black coating. He joyfully took her home to his father.

When his brothers saw them coming they said to their father, "He is bringing that girl home even though she has no teeth."

The father was very disappointed with his youngest son. "You have lost my cattle,

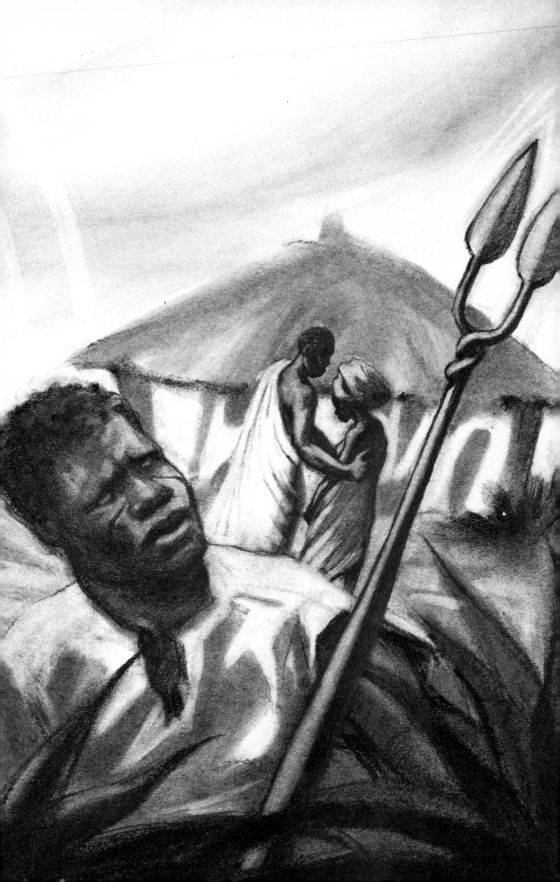

and there is nothing we can do with this girl. I hear she has no teeth and can't eat."

"She does have teeth. Go see for yourself," the son replied.

The father went and asked the girl to open her mouth. He saw for himself that she had teeth.

He called his two oldest sons. "Look, this beautiful girl has fine teeth. It fell to your younger brother to find this out and take her for a wife."

The older brothers were very ashamed and would not look at the girl. Later the village came together for a feast to greet the new girl. Everyone spoke of her beauty and her fine teeth. But the two brothers were always too ashamed to look for themselves.

KENYA

The Sleeping-Mat Confidences

Once long ago Nyankonpon Kwame, the sky god, needed someone to clear his field. The field was overgrown with weeds and itching nettles. The sky god offered the hand of his daughter Abena Nkroma in marriage to anyone who could clear the field without scratching himself where the nettles itched.

Now many men were anxious to marry the beautiful Abena. One after another they came to weed the field. But none of them could keep from scratching. As they failed, everyone laughed at them and made fun of them.

Then Kwaku Ananse the spider decided to try it. But he had a plan. This is how his plan worked. As he was working, the people who passed by on their way to market stopped to greet him. They would ask him how it was that he could clear a field that no one else had been able to clear.

And Ananse would answer, "It's all because of the beautiful Abena that I am working like this. Ah, her arm is like this." And he would slap his own arm where it was itching him and get relief without scratching.

And another person would stop and ask him the same question. And he would say, "Ah, the beautiful Abena. They say her thigh is like this." And he would slap his own thigh where it was itching.

And in this way he managed to clear all the weeds from the field without scratching once.

The sky god was surprised when Ananse finished weeding the field. He couldn't believe anyone had done it without scratching himself. Yet everyone knew Ananse had not scratched.

So the sky god gave the beautiful Abena to Ananse in marriage.

Now Abena was very curious. She often begged Ananse to tell her how he had cleared the field without scratching. One night, as they were lying on their sleeping mats, Ananse told her the trick he had played.

As soon as she had heard the story, Abena became angry. She said, "Tomorrow I will tell my father that you scratched yourself after all."

But Ananse said, "No, you must not tell. This is a sleeping-mat confidence."

"I don't know anything about sleeping-mat confidences," she said. "Tomorrow I will tell my father." And she took her mat

and moved it to the other side of the hut.

Now Ananse was angry. But he soon thought of a plan. When Abena had gone to sleep, he took a gourd of water and poured it over her sleeping mat. Then he went to sleep.

When morning came, he woke her and pointed to the water. "Abena, you are a shameless girl. You have wet your sleeping mat. I shall tell everyone it was true what they said—that everyone who came to the plantation said he was not going to clear a nettle field for a girl who wets."

Abena was very much ashamed and begged Ananse not to tell anyone. But he said he would not drop the matter because she was going to tell her father that he had scratched.

But she begged him, saying she would die of shame. "I will not tell my father if you will not tell what I did."

Ananse agreed. "Both matters will be sleeping-mat confidences," he said.

And to this day the elders say that sleeping-mat confidences are not to be repeated.

GHANA

The First Rain

Long, long ago Ara, the sky maiden, came to earth to marry Nsi. Her father gave her seven male and seven female servants so that she would not have to work. But Nsi would not let her rest.

He ordered her to carry water. He sent her out to collect firewood and to do other tasks. Ara was not used to such hard work and she wept all day.

Her tears made Nsi angry. He did not give her any food until the next day, and even then it was not enough. Then he sent her out to gather more wood. While she was out, she stepped on a thorn and hurt her foot. All day she lay whimpering with pain. Finally by nightfall she made her way home.

Nsi was even more angry. He accused her of loafing all day and doing nothing. That night he made her sleep with the goats. Her foot was so swollen and sore she could not move for five days. Then her foot began to get better.

Then Nsi sent Ara out for water again. At the river, she struggled with the heavy pot and broke it trying to lift it to her head. As the pot broke, a sharp piece fell and cut off her ear. Blood poured out and she began to weep. Then she decided to escape from the cruel Nsi and go back to her parents.

She came to a rope hanging down from the sky kingdom. She began to climb upward, weeping as she went. Halfway up she stopped to rest.

One of her father's servants was out col-

lecting firewood and heard her cries. He rushed to her father, saying, "I have heard Ara's voice weeping near here."

Ara's father sent a number of servants to find her and carry her home. They bathed her, dressed her in fine clothes and made a great feast for her.

Then her father sent his servants to find Nsi. They brought him to the sky kingdom, and they cut off both his ears. "I will send you back to earth earless in revenge for Ara's ear and all the cruelty you visited upon her."

A strong wind rose and blew the weeping Nsi back to earth. On its wings it carried all the cruelty Ara had suffered and all the tears she had shed. Nsi's tears of pain mixed with Ara's, and together they fell to the earth as rain.

Before that time there had never been rain.

CAMEROON

ABOUT THE AUTHOR

Lee Po, a native of Peking, China, has contributed stories and poems to various journals throughout the world. With the collaboration of the well-known children's book author-illustrator William Pène du Bois, he published his first bilingual picture book, *The Hare and the Tortoise and The Tortoise and the Hare,* in 1972.

ABOUT THE ILLUSTRATOR

Carole Byard was born in Atlantic City, New Jersey, and attended the Fleisher Art Memorial in Philadelphia and the New York-Phoenix School of Design. She has received a number of prizes for her illustrations for books, magazines and film strips. She lives in New York City, where she is on the staff of the Studio Museum in Harlem.